WHERE AM I ?

TAMIM IQBAL

Contents

Contents

Preface

Hello folks! I am Tamim Iqbal and I am the author of this book. And the reason of this publication is nothing but to engage brilliant young minds and keep them distracted from virtuality. I truly believe in interacting with the real world. With real people, real situations and real perspective of life. You can simply take it as a way of an ordinary fiction adventure just to unlock your logical thinking and build your situation facing capabilities. I truly hope you enjoy reading this short novel. PEACE

ONE

MOI ET MOI FAMILLE

I am Gordon Clarke, and I am 16, my brother Peter Clarke is 13 and we live in a small town of France named Saint Paul with our parents. Well, we live in a nuclear family with an average house. We actually don't have space for building either a lawn or a backyard because our area of residence is extremely compact. I wish I didn't lived here. Our neighbours are not so friendly but I do have a friend who lives just in front of my house. Marcelo is also 16 and we both study in the same school.

However, my dad is a fabric supplier and often stays out of the town due to work. My mom is a chef at a small restaurant which is situated below the street. She can't spend much time with us due to her job, but she has hired a maid who takes care of us while she and dad are out for work. Juliana is very calm and easygoing. Whenever Peter and I do some mischief, she never tells our mom about it and tries her best to clean up the mess.

Peter is the master of mischief of our house to be honest, but he never falls in trouble because of his innocent looking face. He has a small round face with dark brown hair and tiny blue eyes. I am a tall guy with brown eyes and black hair.

Why am I a normie? I ask myself all the time. My friends call me King Kong just because I am tall. I often hang out with them after school. Stan, Daniel and Allen.

TWO
A MIS HAPPENING

One fresh morning I was having my breakfast with boiled eggs and turkey sandwiches, I get that kind of breakfast only once in a week because our family is financially not so strong.But soon my delightful moment faded away as my brother Peter almost knocked me over from my chair while he was playing with his toy robot.

"Hey you little brat, watch out." I screeched at the top of my lungs. Did I forgot to mention that I am a bit short tempered. That's what all the people say. "Oh! I didn't do it intentionally," Peter said in a low voice acting to be innocent.

"Don't think you will get out of my grab this time," saying that I started to chase him up the stairs.

Peter started to run as fast as possible with a giggle of mischief on his face, but his ankle twisted just when he reached the topmost step and fell down the stairs making a sound of thud through each step he went.

THREE

A SHOCKING MOMENT

Juliana, our maid stood right in front of the staircase. Her mouth dropped open wide, and her hands were on her face. She was frightened. Peter was bleeding his head. I stood at the upper floor, frozen. I didn't even think that this would have happened. Juliana finally ran towards the kitchen and got back with our med-kit. She took out some bandage and called me for help. I rushed down the stairs. Peter was groaning.

I felt so guilty, I wanted to hurt myself, I wanted to be buried deep inside the ground and never to be seen again. I was not tensed of what my mom or dad would say, I was only worried about Peter.

What would happen if something bad happens to him. I tapped him on his back. Was he alright? "Pass me the bandages," Juliana said. I obediently followed her orders. I just wanted to see Peter back on his legs.

Juliana slowly aided the wound and rolled the bandage all round his head. Peter was going unconscious, I noticed.

"Juliana, Peter is going unconscious, do something." Juliana told me to grab a tumbler full of cold water. I immediately went towards the kitchen and poured cold water in Peter's favourite Naruto coffee mug.

I rushed back to where Juliana was sitting crossed legs and handed the mug to her. She cupped her palm and took some water inside it, and sprinkled the water in Peter's face. Peter opened his eyes very low and blinked several times as if trying to say something.

Juliana raised Peter in her lap and went to my mom's room. She put him down on the bedside and drew the curtains blocking the sunlight from entering the room.

She closed the door behind her and instructed me not to disturb Peter for a while. "He will be fine after a quick nap," she said.

FOUR
REALISATION

I went into my bedroom and slammed the door behind me. My throat was heavy with tears, I wanted to scream, I wanted to shout and cry.

I flung myself onto the bed and the thoughts of my brother hovered round my head. My head suddenly felt so heavy. Now I can't have my new hoodie I was supposed to get. Why couldn't I just control myself. After a while I heard a noise of whizzing, it was my mom, she had returned from work.

I immediately recognised the sound of her jalopy and rushed down the stairs. She was already inside the house before I could reach the door.

"Why is it so quiet round here?" My mom murmured. Juliana appeared with a glass of water in front of my mom. I hoped she would not tell mom about anything that had happened today. She won't tell, would she? I questioned myself.

I went into my bedroom and slammed the door behind me. My throat was heavy with tears, I wanted to scream, I wanted to shout and cry.

I flung myself onto the bed and the thoughts of my brother hovered round my head. My head suddenly felt so heavy. Now I can't have my new hoodie I was supposed to get. Why couldn't I just control myself.

After a while I heard a noise of whizzing, it was my mom, she had returned from work.

I immediately recognised the sound of her jalopy and rushed down the stairs. She was already inside the house before I could reach the door.

"Why is it so quiet round here?" My mom murmured. Juliana appeared with a glass of water in front of my mom. I hoped she would not tell mom about anything that had happened today.

She won't tell, would she? I questioned myself.

FIVE

A MOMENT OF FRIGHT

My mom sat on the couch and removed her socks. Juliana helped her with the Apron and the toque Blanche and made a ponytail of her hair.

"Please grab me a cup of tea, I am really tired," my mom told Juliana. She always has to have a cup of tea at every evening.

And if she misses even one day, her temper has to be thrown out on either dad or me, as a matter of fact that Peter is her favourite child.

She sipped her tea and made an uncomfortable noise. I was about to go upstairs but suddenly my mom turned her head towards me and called me with a rather loud voice. "Hey Gordon, where is Peter?"

That question gave me a chill shiver through my whole body. I slowly turned towards my mom and blinked at her several times.

"Would you tell me or not?" she was now being impatient. I opened my mouth to say something, but no words came into my mouth.

I coughed and cleared my throat. I was gulping frantically. What if my mom get to know that Peter fell off the stairs.

My mom was staring at me hard.

"Peter is resting in your bedroom," Juliana finally broke the silence.

"Oh, is he tired, I didn't knew he would even need a rest, he is just like an agile squirrel." My mom laughed sarcastically on her own joke.

Then a silence surrounded the living room. "Well I have to go and finish my homework," I said in a rather croaky voice. "Looks like you had a bad day," my mom said casually.

SIX

AN ALARMING SCREAM

I went upstairs into my room. I was extremely upset. I just rolled in the bed left to right a few times and then went dreaming for hours.

I was awakened by a loud scream which was coming from downstairs. I sat up alarmed.

Was it my mother's voice? She was screaming very loudly.

I heard the voice carefully. No, it was not my mom, it was Juliana. I jumped out of the bed and peeped downstairs from over the banister......

There stood Juliana in front of the kitchen door screeching at top volume.

I went downstairs.......

Juliana suddenly jumped onto the kitchen counter. I was astonished. "What happened Juliana?" I finally spoke. "D..don't move Gordon, d..don't move," Juliana stammered in a frightened voice.

She was pointing her finger towards the kitchen door. I glanced there several times but didn't saw any monster or any pumpkin head ghost.

...But when I looked on the floor, there was a cockroach who was hit hard by Juliana's broom. It was upside down and was moving his tiny hairy legs frantically.

I was rather having pity on that helpless tiny cockroach than Juliana. It was a childish behaviour in my eyes.

....But to be honest, I like to protect Allen from the small bugs which she is afraid of. I took a paper towel from the kitchen counter and picked up the cockroach with one hand and dropped it in the trash can. Juliana finally came off the kitchen counter.

"I almost had an heart attack, phew!" "Well, that was an awful drama," I cried. "Of course it was not, I have a syndrome of getting afraid of bugs and ghosts," Juliana said in a hesitant voice.

"Oh, is it?," I teased. Suddenly I heard Peter's voice from the room. What happened?

SEVEN

A GOOD AND A BAD NEWS

I came sliding through the floor into the room. I was utterly delighted to see Peter sitting on the bed and sipping soup from a bowl.............the doorbell rang suddenly.

Was it my mom? I heard the door open and close followed by a loud sigh.

"Juliana quick come here and bake these fresh Croissants inside the oven, I am hungry."

It was my mom. I heard the noise of the tap water splashing. She was in the restroom. I was tensed at that time. What if my mom gets to know about......you know?

The tap was now closed. My mom entered the room while rubbing her face on a towel.

When her eyes caught the sight of Peter......She glared at me.......I made my eyes look down to the floor, I knew that soon she would know about everything, and I am going to get a never-ending lecture from her. Later that evening she got to know everything as expected...

"How dare you chase your little brother like that," she narrowed her eyes at me. She glared at me hard for a while then she spoke again.

"You are grounded for the whole month." I didn't care, well actually I did care but what other choice did I had.

"Did you thought that I wouldn't know?" My mom glared at me again. "Well let me make this clear to you young man, you better stay away from your brother if you couldn't behave yourself". "You should be shameful for what you have done."

Well, that was a bit too much, I guess. She didn't have to embarrass me in front of everyone, and yeah, the lecture continued forever.

EIGHT

I AM GOING TO DIE

Next day in the afternoon I woke up after a nap and washed my face before I went to check out on Peter.

I peeped from the keyhole and saw him playing video games. Then I slowly entered his room and closed the door behind me silently.

He saw me immediately but pretended as he has not. "I am sorry." I finally spoke. He was still ignoring me. I repeated my words but still he did not payed any attention.

"I know you are upset with me right now, but it was an accident, and I am really sorry for what had happened yesterday." I was miserable. Peter finally stopped moving his controller buttons and the car which was racing on the screen was now moving on its own.

"I am not upset with you." Peter broke the silence. I was shocked him saying that, I mean, if I was him I would have been extremely annoyed with myself.

"I am glad to hear that, Peter." I sat on the bed corner hanging both of my legs and stared at him. He was holding a bowl of cereal in his lap. "Wanna hang out with me." I said in a tiny voice with a forced smile on my face, seeming to be excited.

"Yeah, maybe." He said in a hesitant voice. "Are you interested in a neighbourhood tour." I said eagerly. "Yeah, you can grab my shoes till I get dressed." Peter was in his pyjamas and his hair was undone.

I was now feeling a bit relieved. Peter came out and closed the door behind him. He was wearing a pair of yellow khaki shorts and a printed shirt. He also wore the hat our uncle Matthews had gifted him on his seventh birthday.

He always wore that hat whenever we went for camping or hiking on the vacations. Unfortunately uncle Matthews isn't alive now.

"Shall we go now?" I asked him. "Don't forget to grab the shovel from the attic." I was confused by what he just said. "What did you just say?" "I said what you heard." He replied casually.

I didn't like his tone. He was being obnoxious. "And why you need a shovel in a neighbourhood tour?" I asked him in an unsteady voice.

"You will know very soon." He said. The words were creeping on me. I felt a frightened shiver through my whole body. Something was really off about Peter.

It was a cold evening and he was wearing shorts. And furthermore he was telling me to grab a shovel for a reason I didn't knew about. I helped myself by ignoring the weird thoughts that hovered round my head.

I took the shovel and we both started walking towards the neighbourhood. We passed by old Mr.Lampard's house, then Mrs.Gabriel's house and then Mr.Louise's house. We have a lot of old neighbours from the early nineteenth century. Maybe that's why it's so calm.

Peter was silently strolling through the street and was barely feeling cold. The wind blew violently and I was feeling extremely cold even under my thick sweatshirt.

The street was empty and no one was there till my eyes could see. The tall oak trees' fathomless leaves were moving relentlessly. I was now being a bit alarmed. "I think we should go back." I told Peter. "The weather's not so good." He didn't cared about and continued whistling.

"But I don't think we should." He said in a rather loud voice. "After all you are getting a chance to apologise to me". Said Peter. I was following Peter. I didn't had a clue where he was going. We were now far away from our neighbourhood and it was getting dark.

We had entered the nearby woods. "That's it, I am going back home and telling mom about your weird behaviour." I shouted being frustrated. "You can't go back." Peter's voice had changed. He was sounding like a grown up. The next thing I saw had frozen me at where I was standing. He came into a halt and turned his head towards me. And my eyes nearly popped when I saw his headfirst and then his body turn behind.

His expression changed. He had an evil grin on his face. I could feel the ghoulish vibes coming from him. I could feel the devil surrounding me and slither over my body like a poisonous snake.

I realised that I couldn't move. In all of a sudden I started sweating in that harsh cold weather. The sweat started dripping from my chin to the ground. My sweatshirt was now wet as it soaked the sweat in it.

My heart was pounding hard and I could hear every heartbeat that went rhythmically. Peter was now marching towards me. My heart pounded harder. He came near me, and his eyes were digging inside mine.

He was staring at me hard. I saw his eyes turn pitch black and his canines growing rapidly. Was he turning into a vampire. He silently raised his hand and snatched the shovel from me.

He went a little away from me and then scuffed on a random spot and started to remove the dirt from the ground by using that shovel as if trying to dig. I was astonished. "Uh......h...why are you...dig..ing the g..ground?" I stammered in a low voice.

"I am digging this for you little fella." He sounded awful. "Wh..what...do you mean by...dig....ing for me?" I again stammered in a really tiny voice as I nearly choked. "I am digging your grave." Your soul will be mine. I will kill you for the reason you will never know."

I took a few steps backwards. I turned around before He could say something else.

I started running, but before I could even cross a few yards my legs started aching tremendously. My thighs had a sudden cramp......

I was unable to move either of my legs. And it didn't took long for him to drag and put me alive in that grave. My knees and elbows were bleeding while he dragged me through that rough and uneven forest floor. I was screaming for help, but no one was to be seen. All I could see were pests and dried leaves fallen on the ground.

Peter held me by my right arm and pulled me up and then threw me in that dark grave. My last words came out as a frightened scream. I woke up in a terror. It was all a nightmare.

My heart was racing. The darkness in my room surrounded me. I looked at my alarm clock. It was almost 3:00 AM in the morning and I was the only person awake in the house.

I still couldn't believe that all of this was just a nightmare as it felt so real.

NINE

AN AWKWARD DAY

Next morning I woke up and got dressed. I grabbed my PB&J and rushed towards the door. I wore my newly polished black shoes and took the umbrella from under the porch.

I called for Peter but mom said that he will go school from the next day as he had high fever. Today's weather was unpleasant, it was raining heavily and the storm clouds had gathered together.

The loud and thunderous sound of the lightning was scaring me out a bit. I managed to run and somehow reached my school.

When I walked through the entrance, the guard was staring at me hard and was giving me a weird look. His moustache might have hidden the smile he always had on his face, I thought. He also didn't have an umbrella and his shirt and pants were getting wet.

However, I rushed up the stairs and running through the corridor finally entered my classroom. Everyone was sitting quietly and listening to the teacher.

Nobody was even bothered by seeing me. Was I late? I questioned myself. I also forgot to wear my smartwatch....Everything seemed awkward, as if something bad happened. I sat on the last bench beside Allen. I asked her about the class. She said that she will tell me about that later.

The bell rang exactly at 1:00 PM and everybody started to shove their stuff into their backpacks. I too packed my bag and headed towards the corridor along with Allen.

After a bit walking when we were climbing down the stairs she started speaking. "You asked me about the class earlier."

"Yeah",I said. "Well, today Mrs. Dorothy's husband died and that's why the students were so quiet"."Oh! I am sorry to hear that, I didn't knew about this".

"Mrs. Dorothy must be having a bad time, I guess."Allen sighed. "That's why her eyes were bloodshot."

"Yeah, maybe."

"Do you have any plans today by the way?" "No, why?" "I was wondering if you could come to my house, I am arranging a sleepover tonight."

"That sounds great, are you inviting other people as well?" "Yeah,Only Daniel and Stan are coming."

"When is the time?" "It starts at seven o'clock."

"I have my piano classes at 4:00PM so I can reach there at time, I will catch you later, bye."

"Bye Allen." I was glad that Allen was coming. I had planned all the things we would do in the midnight.

TEN

SLEEPOVER

I reached home and shoved my backpack on the couch and got ready for a hot shower. After sitting in the bathtub for half an hour, I finally came out.

I wore my favourite outfit which was a Yellow T-shirt with black and white designs on it. A black lower with a shade of red patches and putting my earphones I went for sleeping while listening to my playlist of Hollywood songs.

My eyes opened at exactly 5PM, my alarm was ringing nonstop so I had no other choice but go and switch it off. I was feeling sleepy but today I had kept a sleepover so I had to clean the room and bring the DJ speakers from my neighbour, also I had to buy all the snacks for us.

I almost forgot that my Netflix account wasn't recharged and my allowance didn't had enough money for all the things. I checked my pockets, they only had a 10 dollar bill.

I ran to the nearby general store and got some snacks. Then I went to Mr.Louise's house, he lends DJ's to everyone for a fixed price of 5 bucks a night. My allowance was spent as expected.

Now I had no choice but to beg in front of Peter for some money to buy the rest of the things I needed for decorations.

After a long time thinking I had no other option. I went in Peter's room. He was sleeping. I decided to wake him up but then I got stuck with a plan.

I could steal the money from his lame piggy bank and he would never know.

Yes, that was a good one. I tiptoed went passed his bed and silently reached for the piggy bank kept onside his wardrobe. I took the piggy bank and tried to get some money by turning it upside down....but the quarters were making a noise that could wake up Peter.

My eyes then suddenly glimpsed on mom's manicure kit. I opened it to find the pair of tweezers. And I found it. I held the pair of tweezers from one end and after several tries was able to get a hold on a 100 dollar bill.

How did he get this much of money, I thought. Slowly I took it out from the coin slot. I kept all the things on their respective places so that nobody could suspect me.

After closing the door I went upstairs and started to clean all the mess and embellished my room.

I bought a large DJ LED crystal ball which emitted light, party poppers, 3D glasses for the movies and four sleeping bags. All the things costed me around 90 bucks and I had 10 dollars saving.

After about an hour of hard work, everything was fine. Just the Netflix thing was left. A while later I went downstairs and sneaked into my mom's room.

She was snoring. I wished I had a video recorder that time, I wanted to show mom that how she snores while sleeping and never admits it.

Well, it was time for the big step. I opened my mom's purse and grabbed the card holder. I hunted for her credit card and yes! I got it. After going back into my room, I learned from YouTube how to transact money for a Netflix recharge.

After I got my monthly subscription I was over the moon. "The sleepover would be fantastic!" I exclaimed.

ELEVEN

THEY FINALLY CAME

It was 48 minutes past 6 PM and all my friends were about to approach soon. I slid the balcony door and enjoyed the fresh air. The cold breeze made me sneeze three times in a row.

Then suddenly I noticed three people walking over the street. They were Daniel, Stan and Allen.

I rushed down the stairs and opened the door before they knocked. "Welcome guys." I showed them the way towards my room. They entered my room and I followed closing the door behind us.

Allen was looking stunning. I love her dressing sense. She has a very good knowledge of color combinations and wears wonderful outfits all the time whether it is a festive event or any family function.

She was wearing a black top with a pair of light brown cargo shorts. Her pink lipstick and light makeup was looking perfect.

Daniel wore a simple black t-shirt and a ripped blue jeans. He also wore a gold chain and a silver ring. He says it's his style. Marcelo my man had a simple maroon t-shirt and a pair of navy blue jeans.

Stan wore a faded green jacket with a pair of plain grey jeans. His perfect jawline attracts most of the girls in our class.

"I am really very hungry, is there anything to eat?" Daniel and Stan asked.

"Yeah, I have already bought some snacks and drinks before you came, here take this monster drink and these two packets of spicy chicken flavoured chips."

Never mind, my friends are always hungry. I was waiting for someone to notice the decorations and the DJ speakers but nobody saw it. After a while Allen saw the LED crystal ball. She said it was amazing.

Now that Daniel and Stan had eaten, they finally saw the decorations.

I told everyone about the hardship I did for them, and after completing my story, I got a round of standing ovation from my friends.

TWELVE
WHO ARE THEY?

It was nearly 8PM and it was our party time. I took out all the snacks I had from my closet and grabbed the party poppers kept under the pillow.

We had a great time........

After a bit of enjoyment I sat down on the bed switching on the Television. We were about to watch the doctor strange movie and the room was quite settled now.

We tried to make the environment of my room of a cinema hall and of course tried our best to keep our pitch as low as possible because my mom and Peter were sleeping downstairs.

The movie had just started when the Television screen lagged and after a few minutes the screen glitched again. This process repeated several times. "The antenna might be causing this." I told them. "So, what should we do?" Daniel asked. "Two of us have to go to the roof and move the antenna a bit while the other person would make sure that the signal has reached or not."

I told them. "Well this should be easy."

Allen said. "But.....but" I sputtered. "But what?" Allen asked impatiently. "But see outside." I finally blurted out.

Marcelo opened the balcony door and the raindrops came inside the room while the wind blew so hard. The cool breeze gave me a chill shiver. The storm was heavy and the lightning burned a tree far away. It was a harsh moment. Marcelo closed the balcony door and joined us on the bed. We were planning on how to reach the roof without any disturbance.

Finally, after a long discussion, we decided that Daniel and I were going to the roof and Stan will stay inside the room while Allen will notify us with the signal being back.

Daniel and I grabbed the raincoats from my wardrobe and covered ourselves perfectly. We climbed up the stairs barely making any sound.

We both climbed the ladder and opened the vent. I reached the rooftop followed by Daniel. The antenna was tilted. Daniel grabbed the antenna and started to pull it gently towards its former position.

I closed the vent and was about to catch up with Daniel when suddenly my leg slipped and I lost my balance. I fell from the rooftop. I thought that I was gonna die, but I felt no pain when I hit the ground.

I opened my eyes which were closed tightly. I sat up and glanced around, then looked on my left. I saw two people wearing white masks and black suits were standing beside me, they held two thin steel rods each. I noticed that I was laying on a white fluffy substance... Before I screamed, they hit me hard on my head which made me unconscious.

THIRTEEN

WHERE AM I ?

My eyes opened in an unknown place. My head was still aching. I glanced around frantically. I tried to stand but my body didn't have enough stamina to lift me up.

I was frightened. It was totally a bad idea of climbing the rooftop. I thought. I was gasping for breath as if the oxygen level had fallen down or I was in mars or something.

Had the aliens kidnapped me. Weird thought hovered around my head. I never felt so lonely and scared. I shouldn't have kept the sleepover at my house in the first place I thought.

I was literally frightened. I wanted to go home. I wanted to see my mom and dad again. I again glanced around to see someone coming, and that's when I saw a girl who was sitting at the corner of the hall facing down the floor.

I called her. "Hey...are you Allen?" She looked up. No, she was definitely not Allen. Her eyes were bloodshot. She probably hadn't slept for years.

I asked her about the place we were in. She shrugged and said that she didn't know. After talking with that girl I realised that I was not the only one who had been kidnapped but there are several other kids......

FOURTEEN

ARE THEY ALIENS ?

My eyes suddenly caught the sight of Daniel and Stan sitting crossed legs at a distance. I shouted.

"Hey, Stan, Daniel." They both looked back. Yes, they were my friends. I asked them if they knew about Allen. They said that they didn't knew. I was glad to see my friends and was also frightened at that same time.

Suddenly a sound broke the whispers. All of us looked up. A strong beam of light filled that huge hall with light. I now stood up and went towards Daniel and Stan. They pointed their fingers to show me the partition between the boys' and the girls' zone. The partition was not a wall but it was made of several iron rods.

I glimpsed Allen between many girls roaming around. The chattering all over the hall echoed. The boys section had way more people than of the girls.

Every person was as scared as me. In all of a sudden few people with white masks and black suits entered the boys' room just as I saw earlier. They were armed.

I saw different guns in their hands. Their body was fully covered. Everyone was looking towards them. One of the man finally spoke. "I welcome all of you in our dark hall." The man spoke about. A silence surrounded the hall for a while. "We brought you here for a reason; you shall not be frightened."

The man continued. "You shall follow our orders to stay alive." "What kind of joke is this?" A boy finally spoke. His sharp eyes looked into the armed people.

"You shall stay in your limits, or else." The man spoke. "Else what?" The boy argued further. "You want to know little man?" "Of course I want to know because I have a right to know." The man stays quiet for a few minutes and then lifts up his gun. I first thought that he was gonna flinch to scare that boy away, but the little did I know that............

FIFTEEN

CHAOS

He would actually shoot him. The sound of the gunshot echoed followed by a chaos in the room. The boy was shot dead.

Few of the boys showed courage and picked up the iron rods laying on the floor to fight back. But it was of no use.

A few more gunshots and silence again surrounded the room. 4 dead bodies were laying on the floor.

The motionless bodies had blood all over them. The unknown man spoke again. "This is what happens when you break the rules, we will shortly meet you to serve dinner, meanwhile we will have a talk with the girls." They left the room.

All of us were in shock. I mean, we didn't expected this to happen.

SIXTEEN

CONFUSION..... !

"All of you are ordered to sit in a horizontal row, your dinner is going to be served soon. Make 5 rows, in each row 9 boys will be sitting. Maintain a distance between you and the boy sitting in front of you" ......

A strange voice delivered the message. The voice was coming from upwards. I finally spotted the speakers which were attached to the walls of that great hall.

The voice sounded strange. It was like if some robot was talking. I still couldn't get out of the shock. The dead bodies were making me uncomfortable. I wished that someone would take them from there.

The gate opened. 3 people walked in and picked up those bodies making their way out. You guessed right, they were the masked people. Another 3 people entered while the previous ones walked out.

They were holding a pure white cloth. They placed the cloth on the blood which immediately soaked it. This happened in front of us in seconds.

Few of us were scared, some were even crying, while some stood there motionless.

I was still confused about everything and after talking with some other boys I got to know that I am not the only one who has arrived here unknowingly.

There were other several boys who were just puzzled as me. "Hey, would you join me." A random boy called me. I didn't know what to say. "Join you in what?" I asked him. "I want to make a squad in order to fight against the dangerous people here." The boy said.

I was a little confused. "We have to find some way to get out of here. There are gonna kill us for sure if we stay here for long." He added. Before I could say anything, I heard a scream which came from the girls' room. Was it Allen.

It sounded familiar. I rushed near that partition wall, and guess what, it was Allen. They were taking her away. I shouted. "Hey you morons, leave her alone."

The masked people weren't even bothered to glance at me. They just dragged her out of the room. I was shouting continuously. They took her. The next I heard was muffled screams of my beloved.

SEVENTEEN

ENMITY; FORMATION OF GROUPS

"Looks like Jack and Rose are having a bad time here." A boy called out from the back.

I looked behind and saw a muscular boy smiling at me with some other boys surrounding him and they too were big dudes. I was furious at that time.

I went towards them and spoke. "How could you talk like that in this kind of situation?" The other boys were not looking at me in a supportive manner. "Is it even a time to fight guys?" Mike chimed in.

I forgot to tell that Mike was the guy who invited me earlier to join him in his squad like stuff he didn't tell me clearly, I know, it's a bit confusing.

Before anyone could say anything, that big dude punched me on my face. I immediately fell down. "Ow, that hurts." I squealed.

Mike then kicked him on his leg. That big guy punched Mike back, knocking him down. Mike and I both were on the floor holding our cheeks. Stan and Daniel then came.

They first picked us up then pushed that bully away. His companions ran and joined him.

I got up and grabbed a plastic pipe which was kept aside. I threw it towards That big guy with all of my strength. It almost got him, but he managed to dodge it. The big guy then motioned for his cronies to attack Stan and Daniel.

They were punching and kicking each other. Suddenly Mike came up with a wooden chair and smashed it upon that big guy.

I ran towards the bad guys and tried to strangle one of them.

That big guy stood up and gave a flying kick in Mike's chest. Mike fell down. They also got Daniel. They were punching him.

Then suddenly a sound echoed followed by the entry of about 10 masked people.

"The dinner is now being served. Take your seats and enjoy your food."

EIGHTEEN

WHAT'S FOR DINNER ?

We finally stopped fighting. We took our seats and were just about to start eating when I noticed something moving on my food.

On observing carefully I got to see several white slimy worms roaming on my food. "Eww!" I exclaimed.

Everyone looked behind to see what happened. "There are worms on my food." I cried. Another boy cried. "Yes, they're in my plate too." A sudden chaos surrounded the hall again.

NINETEEN

A CHANCE TO ESCAPE

Suddenly some tiny concrete pieces dropped on my head. I looked up and saw the rocky ceiling shaking. "Bend over." I screamed. A heavy rock came tumbling down and fell between the floor.

A red alarm started to buzz violently in all of a sudden. The alarm was screwed to the wall just above the entrance to the hall. Everyone was alarmed.

"Come over here." Mike called. Stan, Daniel and I rushed towards Mike and joined him....

We headed towards the entrance gate. Daniel stepped ahead and tried to open the gate by pushing it but it didn't work, so he tried to hit harder which was of no use either.

Suddenly I glanced at my back and noticed that muscular dude who had a fight with me earlier. He had made a large opening in the wall by breaking it with the help of his other cronies. It was large enough to enter one person at a time.

"Hey guys, look here." I called. We all saw them one after one entering into that large tunnel. Some other boys followed them too, while some of them were covered under the debris. We hurriedly went to catch up with the rest who were getting into the passageway.

Before we could step in a rock hit the floor blocking the opening. The rock fell upon mike's right foot. He screamed violently in pain.

All three of us pulled the rock at our top strength. In that stage of chaos where many boys were still running around, the gate opened and around a dozen masked men entered the hall with guns.

They shouted and ordered us to lay down on the floor. Now was the time of a great rebel...

TWENTY

THE GREAT REBEL

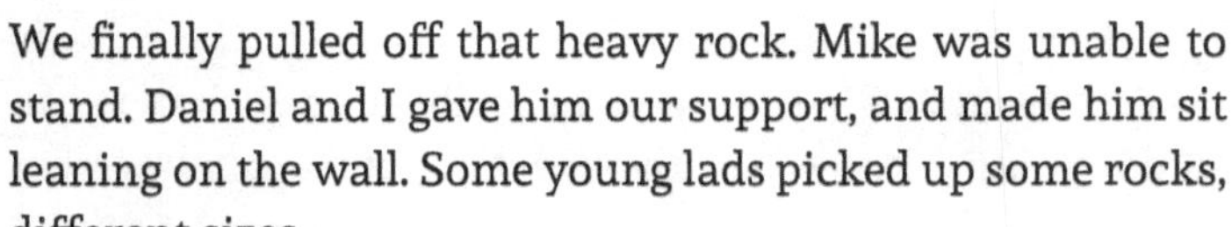

We finally pulled off that heavy rock. Mike was unable to stand. Daniel and I gave him our support, and made him sit leaning on the wall. Some young lads picked up some rocks, different sizes.

They started to throw them away towards the masked men.

The fear of losing their lives had gone. They were fearless, standing with fire fists. Their rages were seeming to destroy the masked men. It was now a game of hunting or being hunted.

I hoped for some miracle to happen. A war had been declared against them. In all of a sudden, a loud noise of gunshots surrounded the crowd.

We picked up Mike and headed into the tunnel. I realised that the passageway was always there as no one made that while we stayed in that dark hall, but why would they make an escape route. I thought. Stan was now following us.

While walking we suddenly bumped into another guy who was running toward the wrong direction. All three of us fell down. I got a fleeting glimpse of his face. His face was similar to Marcelo. Yes, he was Marcelo. I was shocked.

"Hey, Marcelo, you alright." "Gordon." He exclaimed. "What happened why are you rushing into that hell." I asked him.

"Oh, you should also rush back, there's a masked guard who's chasing all the lads.

"Well.........I think I have an idea, but it may or may not work, i don't know. What should I do? "Um, you should give it a try, I mean at the end of the day we may or may not survive."

I sighed. "Let's do this." The boys were rushing back. I made it through them and reached the end.

I saw the guard coming. "Hey, please stop your majesty." The guard stopped immediately.

I continued. "Sir, kindly let us go ahead in exchange of a 10 dollar bill. I know it is unworthy of your acceptance but we want to live. We are kids at the end of the day." I think I won his heart, who knows.

The masked man stood there still, like a mummy. He then got back to his senses and to my horrors, accepted the 10 dollars. I looked up and saw the man step aside and letting us move ahead.

All of us started moving. The gunshots could yet be heard. My heart pounded whenever I took a step ahead. I was sweating. Marcelo was the torchbearer, he led the path.

TWENTY-ONE
DEAD END

Around an hour had passed by now.

Still no sign of an end. "There, see, dead end." Those words from a random teen gave me a chill shiver.

A wall of dirt and rocks had blocked the path. Marcelo dropped the torchlight and pushed hard on the wall, but he fell by the wayside.

Daniel and few other lads stepped forward and joined him. They all pushed together. A crack had formed on that wall. We all backed up.

The wall collapsed and the other end could be seen. We were around 30 boys left. The rest were slaughtered. We moved at a leisurely pace towards the end of the tunnel.

We could see the sun shining brightly. Tall oak trees and a new alluring side of the wildlife.

Robin birds racing in the sky, bald eagles perched on tree branches, Sparrows chirping and a dozen cottontails hopping.

Everything was pleasant except the fact that we were at a height of about a hundred feet above the ground.

Mike could now be considered as a limp and we didn't had enough time as the masked men were probably behind us.

TWENTY-TWO
JUMP OR DIE

Suddenly, Mike shouted. "Guys, there's a river down there, we could jump from here." An awkward silence filled the narrow rocky tunnel. "Oh, what if we die while performing that stunt of yours." A boy said.

"Well according to St.Hans Verde's book of might, a human could survive a hundred and eighty foot free-fall on a water body, and it's practically tested by a Russian prisoner named kai.

Though Mike suggested a risky idea. Many of the boys came forward to leap from there.

A boy named Konami moved to jump when we heard a crowd coming so as to near us. "They are here." Mike uttered low-key."

All the boys there started to panic. Some of them even jumped off.

Stan and Marcelo were holding hands ready to jump off were calling me and Daniel. Mike was leaning on the rocky wall with a solemn face. He was depressed, I could feel the pain in his eyes.

"Quick, come here we have to jump now." I called Mike. He didn't moved. I called again. "Mike, hurry we are by the skin of one's teeth."

I doubted him when he didn't move even this time.

I held him tight and tears filled my eyes. Mike had kicked the bucket. I was grasping a pair of cold forearms.

His lips entirely dried up. The expression of misery had spread over his gleeful face.

The noise of stomping crowd grew louder. They were going to catch us now. In all of a sudden someone hauled me from my back forcefully which made fall from there.

TWENTY-THREE

WHERE AM I, AGAIN?

My eyes opened near a riverbank. I swiftly sat up and looked around frantically.

Where are the other boys, where are Stan, Daniel and Marcelo? I was distressed. I remembered a glimpse of Mike.

My heart was beating rapidly. I was alone in an anonymous site. Some huge leafless holm oaks and cork oaks surrounded me.

I stood up and removed all the dirt sticking on my pants. My throat was dehydrated as I was thirsty for the last few hours.

I could spot some Banyan trees at a distance with extensive aerial roots. A snake could be camouflaged there. Who knows? I moved over the dried leaves and weeds. The forest floor was covered with countless bugs and herbs.

A wooden log was lying down a few yards away. I was nervous as several wild animals could be around.

Maybe a brown leopard was keeping an eye on its prey, and the hunt would be unknown.

Everything was so hushed that I could hear my own breath.

Suddenly I noticed smoke arising at a distance. I darted through all the trees and made it near the campfire where the other boys were warming their hands by the fire.

TWENTY-FOUR
THE HARDEST TRUTH

"Hey, why do you guys left me near the riverside." I asked them. "Gordon, come here and have a seat first."

Daniel stood up, came near me and made me sit near the campfire.

"Why are you all so calm, I mean they are probably behind us." I said in a low voice.

"Don't worry, we are safe now." We are far enough from that hell." Konami said. Konami was Marcelo's cousin.

I searched for Stan and Marcelo but they were nowhere around.

"Hey Daniel, where's Stan and Marcelo? I asked. He told me that Stan, Marcelo and some boys had gone to grab some fruits to eat.

"There are plenty of figs and blueberries around." He said.

"Where's Mike by the way?" That question gave me chills. I saw a glimpse of his face which almost made me cry. Tears filled my throat and made it so heavy.

"He is g..gone forever............"These words could only come out from my mouth.

"Who has gone forever?"

"Mike, he is dead, up on that tunnel," I said. "Who Mike?" Daniel asked me as if he doesn't know. "Are you kidding me, is this even a time for your lame jokes?" I was devastated. How could Dan act so unknown.

After a moment of silence he finally said. "I don't know Gordon what is wrong with you but there was no one named Mike up there with us, i don't know what you are talking about."

My mouth dropped opened, did he just said that Mike didn't existed the whole time.

Then who was the guy I saw up there in that tunnel. Was I hallucinating. That means, all that I saw was a lie. Just then, I saw Stan and Marcelo coming with a handful of berries and figs.

"Hey, Gordon, you are here, good to see you." Stan said while sitting on the wooden log.

I asked him the same question about Mike, and when he said that he didn't knew about any guy named Mike, I was speechless.

Am I going psycho. I was shocked and scared. I was feeling dizzy. I thought that I was gonna fall down.

My eyes were about to close when Konami came and splashed water on my face. I somehow managed to sit again and had some berries.

After a long time, I drank a mouthful of water. The river water tasted a little bit salty, but that should work for now.

TWENTY-FIVE

SHE IS HERE

Then came A boy shouting and said "The girls, they are here." I stood up immediately. "Is Allen there?" I asked.

I moved forward in hope to spot the face of Allen among the other girls.

My eyes then caught the sight of a girl with blonde hair and green eyes. "Allen." I shouted at the top of my lungs.

She saw me immediately and ran towards me. She hugged me so tight that i nearly choked.

Both of us were so glad to see each other. I held her tight and just opened my mouth

to say something when suddenly a thumping sound made all of us move our heads.

They were here......I knew the masked morons would catch up and so I warned others about it.

"Sit down all of you and keep both of your hands behind your head." A masked man ordered us.

Everyone followed their orders. "We are the official firing squad assigned by our master, and we are sent to encounter all of you." They continued. Everyone panicked...

"Please don't kill us." Marcelo begged in front of them, but it was of no use. The man in the lead kicked hard on his shoulder which made Marcelo fall on his back.

No one uttered a single word. Everybody had realised that we are getting doomed.

All of the men loaded their magazines and placed their finger near the trigger.

TWENTY-SIX

A MIRACLE

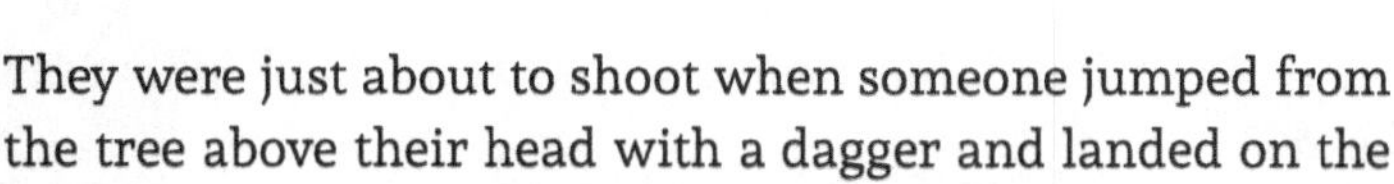

They were just about to shoot when someone jumped from the tree above their head with a dagger and landed on the first man's shoulder, he stabbed him below his throat.

A loud wail followed by. The unknown man leaped upon the second guy and slaughtered him ruthlessly.

The other two lifted their gun but it was too late. The man threw his dagger so hard that it ripped the man's chest. The last guy shot a bullet but the man managed to dodge it and broke his neck.

What I just saw was unbelievable. Another masked man who appeared out of nowhere killed four armed men in seconds.

Who is he. I needed to know. The man turned towards us and took some steps forward.

He looked at me and then at the silent bunch of teens. He then snapped his fingers and four other men landed on their toes from above our heads.

All five of them were wearing heavy, long and black robes while covering their faces with scarves.

The man took his dagger and rubbed it against his robe to clean the blood.

He took a few steps towards me. I was scared. Was he gonna kill me? Was the first thought I thought. The man had sharp green eyes and some wrinkles underneath them.

He revealed his face to me. I was shocked. The man whispered something in my ear and then told me to stay silent and not to tell anybody about anything he said to me right now in my ears.

I couldn't believe my eyes.

The man then took a few steps backwards and announced, "I am Vincent, but you can call me Mr.Vincent, and I am here to save you." He sounded just like our principal on annual day ceremony giving a speech. "I know you all are afraid, but you have to trust me and follow my lead.

"What a liar," I muttered. "Well it's getting dark in the woods and many wild animals could be around. He added.

"Follow me before it gets too dark."

He started walking towards the West. All of the kids followed along with him. I still couldn't believe any of that either I saw or heard. To me it was just impossible.

Dried leaves crunched underneath my sneakers. The cool breeze made the autumn leaves rustle. The sun was about to set.

Suddenly he motioned us to stop. I could see a wooden house at a distance. He went a little ahead and unlocked the door. "Come in." He instructed us to enter one at a time because the door was very narrow.

I stepped in and saw a dusty hall filled with some old furnitures and stuff.

The floorboard creaked under my sneakers. The hall was big enough to fit over twenty people. The window beside the door was shattered.

I could see an old wooden armchair and a broken mirror leaned against the side wall. The couch had a broken arm and the floor seemed as if it had been not cleaned over a decade. I sneezed four times in a row.

Mr. Vincent then stepped ahead of me and announced, "I will be heading towards the North after a while with my companions, till then you can settle yourselves down."

We were a total of sixteen people- eight boys and eight girls.

I trotted over to Mr. Vincent and said, Excuse me uncle Mathews, I almost blurted out these words out of my mouth.

You guessed it right. It was my dead uncle Mathews who I thought had passed away three years ago.

He had whispered to me earlier to stay quiet and to not reveal his real identity.

I asked him that how is he alive in front of me if he died three years back to the whole world and to me. "Could you explain me?" He paused for a bit and started. "I know it's hard for you to believe what you saw but I never died."

What did he mean by that. "You see, I somehow survived in the war and spent two years of my life in some kind of secret underground basement. I was pale back then; loneliness had killed my sleep. I could barely move. My body too abandoned me. I didn't even had hope, but one day few people rescued me from there and healed me before they welcomed me in their secret assassin universe. That's all I could remember." That was a lot for me to digest. So, I decided to change the subject. "Uncle Mathews, do you mind helping me and my friends to find our homes. We live in Saint Paul."

TWENTY-SEVEN
A NEW HOPE

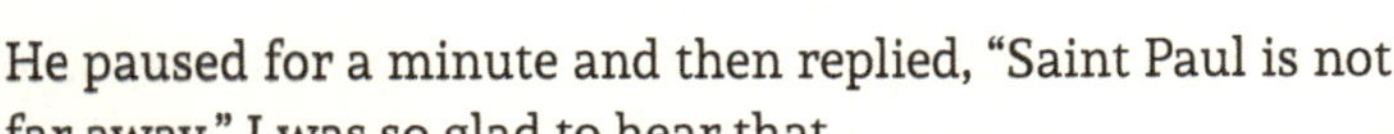

He paused for a minute and then replied, "Saint Paul is not far away." I was so glad to hear that.

"Walk towards the west until you find a stream. He said. "You have to cross the stream and have to walk through the woods until you finally see a wall made up of dirt.

You have to climb up and continue your journey until you spot the arrow shaped plank that leads into Saint Paul.

I thanked him and walked toward my friends. "Hey, guys, I think I found the way back to our homes."

"You are joking right?" Daniel said while exchanging uncertain glances with Stan.

"No, not at all, I just got to know the path, Mr. Vincent told me."

"Are you sure what he said is right?" Allen asked me. "We don't want to get in a major trouble, do we?"

"What if we lost our way?" Stan asked.

"You guys got a point but what other choice do we have."

Suddenly someone grabbed my shoulder from my back. It was Marcelo.

"Hey what are you up to?" "Um...we were just trying to figure out how to get back to our homes." I said.

Marcelo sat beside me letting a long sigh. "I guess we are trapped here forever." He said in a low voice.

That evening uncle Mathews left. Before going, he instructed me to not move out of the house until tomorrow morning because it could be dangerous. He basically warned me of some wild creatures roaming at night would have a feast on me. Yeah right.

Uncle Mathews also left some bread loaves and raw honeycomb for us to eat before our journey. Is he a dietitian or something? I asked myself. I hoped for something better to eat. I scolded myself for being such a lame person.

I woke up tomorrow morning with a beam of sunlight pouring the hall with light. I shielded my eyes and sat up.

I saw Marcelo and Allen standing. "What happened?" I asked. They were looking so stressed.

"They all.....left." A low utter escaped his throat." I gaped at them in shock.

I glanced at the empty hall, nobody except me and my friends.

"How could you let them?" I was so miserable. I saw Stan, Daniel and Konami sitting solemnly leaning on the wall. A moan escaped my throat. I grabbed the loaf of bread lying beside me and stood up.

I pushed that bread loaf in my mouth and headed toward the doorway.

"Where are you going Gordon?" Stan asked. "Everyone follow me." I said. "We are going back to our home."

The five of them stared at me uncertainly. "What happened?" I asked them.

"Are you sure that you will lead us to our home." Allen said in a trembling voice.

"We don't have a choice, do we?" They stared at me a few more seconds and then walked out of the house.

It was early morning and the robins chirped happily. The sunlight shone brightly.

The cold breeze made me shiver. I closed my eyes tight and inhaled the fresh air and let out a long sigh.

The journey wasn't going to be easy.

Allen handed me her compass. I read the directions carefully and moved forward.

Our journey had begun. We walked through tall trees of leafless oaks and dried maple trees. The shrubs led into a straight line. I was hoping to spot the stream that uncle Mathews had told me about. It had been a long time and still no sign of a stream. "Hey, what's that?" Daniel said. "Is that a stream?" Allen screamed.

Yeah it was indeed, I ran toward the direction they had pointed. "We found it." I uttered being delighted.

The stream was crystal clear. All of us drank the clear, cold flowing water. The stream bed had many colourful features. Tiny rocks tumbled over and dropped on the stream. We washed our face and moved on. Slowly, we crossed the rapidly flowing water body. Konami almost tumbled down.

"Watch out!" I exclaimed. We continued walking. A small cottontail hopped over my foot.

I was about to scream. I scolded myself for being such a scaredy-cat. Another long hour of walking we finally spotted the dirt wall. "The dirt wall, we have reached the dirt wall."

Yes, we are so close. I suddenly had a throbbing headache, I glanced ahead and saw the dirt wall. We were following the right direction.

It was too tall to climb so Marcelo and I together pushed it and it collapsed. I saw a sign board which read. -**Welcome to Saint Paul-**

Tears rolled down my eyes. "We are back, I am going to see my parents again." Allen cried. We hugged each other.

I wiped my tears and took a few steps forward. The moment I stepped ahead; a gust of cold breeze carried a strong aroma of fresh lavenders to my nose. What a feeling it was.

I remembered the street. - **Le Dazzle Restaurant** - I saw my mom's small restaurant.

I was so glad, my brother Peter and my mom & dad are probably waiting for me in front of the doorway.

The long walk through the woods and all the struggles throughout our journey seemed worth it now.But in all of a sudden my smile faded

TWENTY-EIGHT
NOT AGAIN!

There stood the masked men. Four muscular masked men blocking the street.

"This can't be happening." I muttered in a low voice." My voice barely escaped my throat.

I could hear all of my friends gasping behind me. "How did you follow us?" Marcelo finally broke the silence.

No reply.

They stood frozen. Then suddenly, the man in the middle raised his left hand and pulled his mask off.

Me and my friends stared at him in horror. "U.... uncle Mathews?" He then motioned the short guy beside him and the other guy on his left to shove their masks off. My chin touched the ground as they followed, there stood Peter and Mike with an evil grin on their faces.

"Welcome to the world of dead" ......

www.ingramcontent.com/pod-product-compliance
Lightning Source LLC
Chambersburg PA
CBHW031334130726
47988CB00007B/3133